WINTER KING,
SUMMER QUEEN

WRITTEN BY MARY LISTER
ILLUSTRATED BY DIANA MAYO

Barefoot Books
Celebrating Art and Story

In the beginning, long long ago, the sky was split into two kingdoms. One kingdom was warm and sunny. The other one was cold and dark.

Land of the Flaming Sun

The warm kingdom was called the Land of the Flaming Sun, and the cold kingdom was called the Land of Icy Darkness.

In the Land of the Flaming Sun lived Queen Goldenlight.

Her eyes were like blazing stars.

She wore the moon in her crown.

Her smile was like a sunbeam.

Her hair was like flaming fire,

and her cloak was made of
galaxies of a million, tiny,
glimmering, shimmering stars.

Her palace was made of bright
white light.

Queen Goldenlight had lots of friends.

Master Moonbeam

Sunshine Sally

Far away across the sky, King Icicle ruled in the Land of Icy Darkness. No one messed around with King Icicle.

He was a fierce frost giant.

His heart was made of snow and frost.

His eyes were like ice splinters.

On his feet were spiky icicle boots.

He wore trousers made of glaciers and a huge, snow-blown cloak.

King Icicle's companions were quite different from Queen Goldenlight's. They were:

Mr. Thunderbolt

Miss Twister

Harry Hurricane

Danny Drizzle

Anatya Monsoon

Philippa Freezo

Queen Goldenlight and her friends liked to warm the
Earth, sending light and heat to all the men, women
and children. They played games and sang songs all the
time. While they played, the birds sang, the bees buzzed
and the butterflies danced.

But King Icicle and his companions were gloomy and cold. No one said "hello," they just said "Brrrhhh!" They didn't sing songs or play games. They just played ice music, but that made the land even colder.

King Icicle's favorite sport was to send storms down to the Earth.

Thunder boomed –
crash, crash!

Snow fell –
shiver, shiver!

The people on Earth got so cold that they all turned
into snow men and snow women and snow babies.
The birds stopped singing, the animals shivered and the
fish froze in the ponds and rivers. Everyone was very
unhappy.

When Queen Goldenlight looked down at the Earth and saw how cold everyone was, she said, "We must do something!"

To help the fish, she sent a magic fish.

To help the birds,
she sent a magic bird.

To help the animals,
she sent a magic hare.

And she gave each of them a ray of endless sunshine to
help them in their task.

The bird flew around the Earth, the hare bounded across the frozen land, and the fish swam bravely through the icy rivers.

And in and out of the water, air and earth they wove rays of endless sunshine, making a beautiful stripy rainbow.

When King Icicle saw the rainbow he
was furious. He sent storms to blow it down.

Winds blew – phew, phew!
Lightning crackled – flash, flash!
Thunder boomed – crash, crash!
Snow fell – shiver, shiver!

But nothing happened.

Land of the Flaming Sun

Then Queen Goldenlight asked her friends to sing a song to make the rainbow grow. So everyone started to hum. And as they hummed, the rainbow grew and

Land of Icy Darkness

grew until it became a huge bridge between the Land of
the Flaming Sun and the Land of Icy Darkness, right
over the Earth. It was beautiful!

When the people in the Land of the Sun and the people in the Land of Ice saw the rainbow, they all wanted to run up it. Even King Icicle's heart started to melt when he saw the rainbow. He wanted to climb it! So up he ran in his pointy icicle boots.

As he ran, the boots started to melt, squelch, squelch, squelch! And King Icicle actually laughed! At first it came out as an icy cackle, then it crackled and cracked and began to melt, until it had become a really jolly, happy chuckle. Ha ha ha! Ho ho ho!

At the top of the rainbow, King Icicle met Queen Goldenlight. "May I have the honor of a dance?" he asked, bowing low.

"I shall dance with you if you can answer this riddle,"
the Queen replied.
"Red, orange, yellow; blue, indigo, violet, green,
The King can dance over it, and so can the Queen!
Storms cannot destroy it, although their power is great.
Answer me this riddle before I count to eight!"

Of course, King Icicle answered the riddle. He and Queen Goldenlight danced and danced and everyone danced with them. Down on Earth, the snow melted away on all of the people and they danced too.

Afterwards, the King and the Queen came to an agreement. From then on, all of the weather could share the Earth. The King became winter, and he was to look after the Earth for six months of the year. The Queen became summer, and she was to look after it for the other six months. They were to

share everything, so that we have a mixture of cold and warmth, sunshine and rain, light and darkness. And now, we do! But sometimes, just very occasionally, King Icicle forgets himself and sends out too many of his cold spirits. And that's why we get storms and hurricanes.

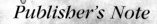

Publisher's Note

This story was originally written for a literacy project for 4 – 7 year-olds at England's West Yorkshire Playhouse and was designed to extend children's vocabulary, use of language and sense of story structure and characterization. There are numerous ways in which the text can be used to explore and enhance children's understanding of the story, both in the classroom and at home. Please visit the Barefoot Books website, www.barefootbooks.com, for an array of teaching ideas and crafts suggestions. From creating a seasonal collage to building vocabulary, there is a rich offering of activities online for children to enjoy and learn from.

To my mother and father, who are my favorite parents — M. L.
To Jake, for all your love and support — D. M.

Barefoot Books
2067 Massachusetts Ave
Cambridge, MA 02140

Text copyright © 2002 by Mary Lister
Illustrations copyright © 2002 by Diana Mayo
The moral right of Mary Lister to be identified as the author and
Diana Mayo to be identified as the illustrator of this work has been asserted

First published in the United States of America in 2002 by Barefoot Books, Inc.
This paperback edition first published in 2007

This book was typeset in Garamond Infant 19 on 24 point
The illustrations were prepared in acrylics on hotpress watercolor paper

Graphic design by Judy Linard, London
Color separation by Grafiscan, Verona, Italy
Printed and bound in Singapore by Tien Wah Press (Pte) Ltd
This book has been printed on 100% acid-free paper

Paperback without CD ISBN 978-1-84686-080-5
Paperback with CD ISBN 978-1-84686-009-6

1 3 5 7 9 8 6 4 2

The Library of Congress cataloged the first hardcover edition as follows:

Lister, Mary.
The winter king and the summer queen / written by Mary Lister ; illustrated by Diana Mayo.
p. cm.
Summary: Queen Goldenlight and King Icicle rule two very different kingdoms, but they learn to share their influence
so that the Earth will have six months of summer and six months of winter.
ISBN: 1-84148-357-5
[1. Seasons—Fiction. 2. Summer—Fiction. 3. Winter—Fiction. 4. Sharing—Fiction.] I. Mayo, Diana, ill. II. Title.
PZ7.L6955 Wi 2002
[E]-dc21
2001007576